The Nightwatchgirl of the Moon

A Poetry Anthology for ilf's Silver Anniversary

Edited by Ian Duhig

ilf25

ILKLEY LITERATURE FESTIVAL 1973 - 1998

Published by **ILF Books**, The Manor House, Ilkley, LS29 9DT

© Text: Contributing Authors
© Cover Design: Neil Palliser
Production: Ian Daley

ISBN: 0 905199 02 2

Printed by FM Repro, Liversedge

Ilkley Literature Festival is grateful for support from:

SUPPORTED BY
THE NATIONAL LOTTERY
THROUGH
THE ARTS COUNCIL
OF ENGLAND

Yorkshire & Humberside
A R T S

West Yorkshire Grants
WYG

City of
BRADFORD
METROPOLITAN DISTRICT COUNCIL

Contents

Introduction

This anthology comprises work by the Judges and Winners of the ilf Poetry Competitions form 1994-1997 and by this year's three Judges, Winners and Runners-Up. Given the Ilkley Festival's record of appointing some of the best poets living in Britain as adjudicators, this book cannot fail to be interesting on that count alone. However, in their turn they have chosen wonderful poems to honour with prizes as the reader will quickly appreciate. In fact, such was the pressure on space that John Latham, eligible twice as 1995's Winner and Third Prize this year, is only represented by the poem which earned the greater honour.

The major theme of what follows is the many aspects of love and our title is from a marvellous poem, the 1997 Winner, Louise Goulding's *Nine Lives*. Robert Graves argued that all true poetry is in service of a universal triple-goddess, anciently incarnated in the phases of the moon. Goulding's phrase seems to give her a new, modern dimension, one particularly appropriate for ilf as it enters its silver age. Often we boys tend to fool about a bit in our efforts to connect, but Melvyn Rust's *Anticipating Next Week's Lunch* fixes a specimen out of his depth with women. Stephanie Bowgett and Kathleen A. Karlis, however, capture the disturbing power of sex itself, while Dorothy V. J. Pope deals with unsisterliness, hatred in a mask. I was also struck, aptly, by this year's Winner of the Yorkshire Prize, *Stone* by Louise Holmes, which reads like a chant and works like a charm. In contrast, U. A. Fanthorpe, 1997 Judge and one of the most consistently excellent of English poets, shows us London eating itself, stone and brick torn out for cars. Susan Brown's *Leaving You Behind* writes of love's loss, alienated in a German Language where she can't find the word for pavement. This suggestion of homelessness is picked up in this year's Winner, Bruce Barnes' *No north or south*. The past is his foreign country, invading ours with fierce ghosts, a brood of Ludd ambushing ramblers and smashing their compasses. Their strength is that they are allies of Nature and they find a fit symbol of Her desecration: "smoke/from mills presumed to crop the moon."

The moving spirits behind this moon crop were Alice and David Porter and my thanks are due to them as are those of all who enjoy it. Happy Anniversary ilf.

Ian Duhig

Free Improvising Musician Drops Frying Pan

Crash of it so random, depends
on all sorts: type of floor. Type
of frying pan. Position of the bacon and the eggs.

I'll incorporate it into the gig tonight,
somehow. Filtered through the day, of course,
the things I haven't done yet,

sounds I've not heard. Tonight's music
starts now, nice and early, this morning,
frying pan in mid air really the start of it,

start of all improvisation, the music
not yet heard, the bacon not yet

in a pattern on the floor, the eggs
running, running to keep up

with themselves. Keeping up with itself:
the music not yet played, not yet heard.

Ian McMillan
Judge, 1995

Children of the Enlightenment

I have heard the old wives say
that the yew is a death tree. Cows
will not eat it, nor ever
stray to the grave-yards where it stands.
But we have risked the dark, tamed it. Clipped
like a poodle, it becomes the maze
we tread with measured steps
admiring the pom-poms
on our pink satin slippers.

The man in the hot-air balloon above
our heads, light as spun-sugar
can see the logic
the symmetry. He smiles at me
doffs his cocked hat. I serve him
plump breasts on a bed
of Brussels lace. He knows
that my skirt is counter-balanced
to lift at the flick of a finger
and that knickers are not yet invented.
I know the bulge in his breeches
is padding, but I need the perfection
of his calves in silk stockings.

The air we breathe is blown
from the mouths of babies with wings.
Fat and golden, like pascal lambs, they frame us
with corpses of gilded birds
swags of acanthus, bunched grapes.
And when we dance, we dance to the music
of synthesis, equilibrium.
Sublime, we dance the new figures.
Describe them in hedges of yew.

Stephanie Bowgett
Winner, 1994

The Houseboat

'Did Dick Blackstaff do it?
Is he the fucker we want?'
We banged on the hatch of that houseboat,
under a blood-red moon,
while a police siren weaved among the flats
and a dog howled till a shot rang out.
But we heard no sound from that cabin,
no whisper, or muffled step,
so we banged again, and shouted
'Blackstaff, if you're in there
come out and clear your name.'
And these words rang over the water
to the wreck of the tanker
where the kids hung out in summer
but now was as bare as a crag.
And the houseboat rocked, as the wind
whipped up the incoming tide,
and brought with it the smell of curry
from 'The Star of Malibar'.
'Tell Blackstaff there's a bullet
waiting for his skull', we shouted
before jumping back to land
and cramming in Jack's Audi
for the short ride home.

Matthew Sweeney
Judge, 1994

The K.O. Culture

Differences were settled with a punch,
Though crack of fist on jaw would always seem
Too sharp, the sound of speeding billiard-balls
Colliding with abrupt and bony *clack*;
No real punch on the jaw could sound like that.
But these encounters happened on the screen,
And we believed in some platonic sense,
That those right-hooks were real, not like our own
Wild swings in back street, bar or football-stand,
Which missed completely or smashed up your hand,
And hurt the striker far more than the struck.

Our heroes and exemplars might be tough
Stetsoned cowpokes wearing neckerchiefs,
Leathery chaps in leather chaps and spurs,
Whose fist-fights were conducted in the bars
Of honky-tonk saloons; or they could be
Gangsters in fedoras, just as quick
With uppercut or haymaker as gun.
But these were not the only ones who punched;
Even Catholic priests could use their mitts.
You hardly ever saw a film in which
No character got walloped on the chin.

Even debonair society dudes,
When cross, or crossed in love, knocked culprits cold.
Remember them? Tuxedoed, brilliantined,
The Roberts – Taylor, Young, Montgomery –
William Powell and Melvyn Douglas, all
Capable of flattening a cad
As coolly as they lit a cigarette
In frothy comedies. It's what they did,
And what we did as well, or not so well,
Or tried our best to do if we were mocked,
Insulted, wronged in any way. We socked.

And, as I've said, we often missed or bust
Our fist on ivory skull, or else we found
Ourselves entangled with the adversary,
Undignified and rolling on the ground.
Absurd. And yet one sometimes heaves a sigh
To insult with a quick right-cross. Or tried.
Surely better than the baseball bat,
Machete, knife or, worst of all, the gun
That now replace the fist, off-screen and on –
If things have ever truly been like that.

Vernon Scannell
Judge, 1996

At The Death Bed of Desperate Dan

Fingers graze and fidget in his face's stubble-field.

Difficult to credit, this beached whale on the bed
gravel in his windpipe, engine almost failed,
once – a single mighty breath –
blew a stricken liner from New York to Liverpool.

A solitary, innocent – as all true saints must be.

Never, desperate, easy to outfox,
unbeliever in Man's duplicity
he won through always
bullets bouncing off his chest
swatting them away: "Durn them pesky flies".

This massive chin, scoured daily with a blowlamp
the essence, measure of the man.

His good deeds legion, prodigious, botched:
carried a log cabin through a tottering mile
careful as a blindfold tight-rope walker,
sighed it to his knees, lowered it into place,
sneezed it into smithereens;

dived, chin grinning, from the Golden Gate bridge
to show frightened youngsters
how to swim,
flooded San Francisco with the tidal wave.

This forehead moist and cool as sunless granite.

Life has grown too subtle for this legend,
blundering the sidewalks
frowning at screen-flicker
wondering why folk ignore his outstretched hand,
emasculated in this electronic age
where laser guns can frizzle him, still pondering.

He lies in coma, skull pierced by the spear
he hurled into a cloud to puncture drought.
At the time it struck him
gazing proudly into rain
it had circuited the world eleven times.

Dawn-light glints off a frozen mountain-top,
these pines across the northern face still growing

John Latham
First Prize, 1995

Cigarette Cards

He was a man of the thirties:
motorcar assembly track
more than fifty hours a week,
plenty of overtime, one of the lucky ones.

Cigarette cards, complete series,
he collected and gummed
precisely into albums
or in numerical order, stacked
in old ten-packets,
Wills' Wild Woodbines and Players' Weights,
the people's smoke,
hand cupped and dragged,
the one furtive gesture against the Factory Act.
Like stills from dated movies,
they frame the glamour of our parents' lives:

Cricketers of 1934
young heroes with glossed
middle-aged haircuts;

Famous Footballers,
see, the left-half Dad brushed past
at the tobacconist's;

Tennis Champions,
from a Wimbledon of eye shades, discreet
flannels and long, cream skirts;

Radio Celebrities,
in bow-ties, looking the cat's whiskers,
faces shining like waxworks;

Film Stars,
from black and white movies,
unreal in rouge-cheeked disguise;

And

International Airliners,
Whitworth flying-boat,
adventuring the Imperial sunset;

Railways,
trans-Europe express,
luxuriating towards the final excess.

And best of all, those

Motorcars,
continental limousine, open
tourer, drophead
coupe, V-8 22 with running-board
and the SS Jaguar 2°-litre saloon –
the one he stroked with pride
on the Final Line, fingers
and thumb astringent from thinners,
paint and tobacco-stained,
gripping the soft, tapered sable brush
gently as a fresh woodbine
to draw the steady stripe of gold or red,
a delicate sporting flourish,
along the black cellulose streamlined
body which he never entered,
never took for a mad spin,
never risking the crash.

They accelerated by, the heydays,
left him behind
with *Air Raid Precautions* for a phoney
war, when he lined
up for a B2 medical, the soldier's
fag trickling smoke along his khaki
sleeve through a drill-parade of years
helping crack divisions,
the front-rack *Regiments of the British Army,*
move forward, while he patrolled
the edge of the battlefield
and survived, one of the lucky ones,
to return to a forty-hour week
and king-sized filters advertised with gold-
braid cuffs and manicure. He smouldered
on, retired from work to talk
of nothing else, stopped smoking, just
to sit, dreamless, empty hands clutching,
flexing, drawing firm lines
under his opinions,
tapping his knuckles
and easing a finger proud from the fist
as if to offer you his packet.

David Duncombe
First Prize, 1996

Widening the Westway

Torched, they might have been, in another country
Because the wrong people lived in them;
Or, in quieter times, in homelier places,
Left to slither modestly back to earth.

But this is London. There are guide-lines.
Houses are groomed for a protracted ending.

Some house-man has been on his rounds, diagnosing
The slow-motion stages of a terminal event.
Amputate, he prescribed. First went the more portable shrubs,
The carpets, fittings. Lastly, the people.

Then experts came. They blinded each window
With hardboard, extracted knockers and bells like teeth;
As nurses raise screens in wards to island the dying,
They erected eight-foot boards to segregate.

(And someone has aerosoled *Save us* and *Help*,
Help and *Save us*, along the new wood).

An avenue-full of confident thirties semis,
Twin-gabled, porched, with double mock-Tudor chimneys,
Who shopped at the Army and Navy, golfed in Ealing,
Dentists, dog-walkers, Dry Fly drinkers – that sort of house.

Now they tremble together, W12 Samsons;
Rooftops flayed of tiles are all you can see.
Tomorrow men in heavy duty yellow jackets
With JCBs will rubbish the garlanded plaster.

(And the forsythia gamely still in flower,
And the houses opposite watching speechless
Like aristos brought too soon in their tumbrils,
Watching the load before them).

That was the way the world marched on.
This may be how it starts. *Atrocity*
Is what we haven't got used to yet.

U.A. Fanthorpe
Judge, 1997

Reading

There's the book.
It is there
On my desk.
I will myself to pick it up.
It is in my hand.

I start to read.
I wish I hadn't
I want to stop,
I will myself to carry on,
I struggle through.

There's the character.
She is there
In my mind,
I want to know what will happen,
I can't stop.

The story unfolds inside my mind,
I start to feel what they feel,
The people on the page
Come alive in my head,
the letters that were bland,
have emotions like me,
the people, on the page
that live, in the book
are with me.

The book ends.
I hold on,
shall I start again,
I force myself to put it down,
the letters gone.

There's the book.
It is there
On the desk,
but inside the characters live on.
They don't stop.

Amy Fidgett
Student Prize, 1997

Nine Lives

From sun to priest to raindrop to lover
to picture to star to cross to sinner
to Hell to now to Heaven and back
and down and round and round
I spin to the sound of death at my back
of the end of the tracks.
No chariots, just a wail
and his smell on my tail.

I
I am the golden light that sticks like honey to the trees
each heavy hazy evening in the orchards of the south.

II
Oh Father Brown, I am not cut out to be a priest.
I get lonely and hungry
and am filled with the ungodly desire to scream.

III
Look, there I am, a brown drop in a puddle
and when the boot comes I leap up and fly.

IV
And now I am in love, at least
until I place my head upon his chest
and hear the beating wings
of the live bird he ate for breakfast.

V
Being a portrait is a very easy life,
They stare at me and I stare back.

VI

I am the nightwatchgirl of the moon
who frightens off the thieves who would carve hunks of cheese
out of my mother's pale creamy thighs.

VII

A wooden crucifix high on a white wall:
arms open, legs shut tight though.
One has to set an example
to the streams of convent girls below.

VIII

The season in Hell was not a good one.
I ate raw man
but shall not dwell on it or them.

IX

And now comes this one.

Louise Goulding
First Prize, 1997

First Aid Class

I kneel there with the head gardener in my arms,
feeling the pulse in his neck the way he touches
leaves in real life, his skin a series of impressions
on calico beside me. Everyone an iridologist
dressing head wounds with the enthusiasm
of the stretched in field hospitals before 1915.

We learn that fainting is merely the rearrangement
of blood, my bronchial tree simply a cameo of me,
but more vitriolic. I am eager to see the cyanosed
around the edges, intuit a cardiac arrest.
Now and then I hear the thrum of a defribulator,
arterial gestures from the past. Handling a rib-cage
over lunch I have a sense of ornament.
Finally we study a handout of unconsciousness,
poison ivy groping at the window panes.

I imagine us meeting under other circumstances,
coy with our intimacy. Then I begin to understand
the way surgeons avoid the resuscitated
in *The Lamb & Flag,* the gardener playing cribbage
something too abstract, why terminology matters:
"terracotta" to "red", "episode" only a dot
on a screen.

We are asked to elevate a limb: the rituals of a sacrament.
The illustrations in the manual mute in savagery
as my hands around those broken varicose veins.

S. W. Rhydderch
Runner Up, 1998

Message from Old Fashioned Baby Sitter to New Man

Arriving
At her assertiveness class
Driving
The bigger car, of course,
She boasted -
Boasted! –
That you were home
Doing the ironing
While minding both the girls
And James.

This on your half day from the practice
Where two female partners
Are off on
Pregnancy leave.

She looked so carefree,
Energetic, unlined, young.
You looked so tired,
So put upon, My Love.

I got Pip's weekend homework done,
(Does she always call you John?)
Heard Lucy read,
Then after game and story each,
While cuddling James,
Tucked them all up
With looked-for kiss
On each one's peachy cheek.

I've done her bloody ironing
Starting with your shirts when fresh,
The children's next,
Then hers.
I polished up your well worn shoes
Then settled down
With buttons and with mending thread
I brought from home.

Your every shirt is now entire
All pocket linings sound
And I've washed up in case
That fell to you.

I'll offer to go home by cab.
"No, no!" she'll say. "John doesn't mind.
He'll run you home."
I'll not demur.

And on the way
In the bigger, roomy car
We'll pause a while
And I'll make a new man of you
The old fashioned way, My Love.

Dorothy V.J. Pope
Runner Up, 1998

Anticipating Next Week's Lunch

He takes her out for lunch and drinks
Approximately once a week
But that's as far as he dare go –
They're just good friends or so he thinks.

They talk about their 'other' life
She has a daughter, he two sons.
She's a single parent now –
He's told her all about his wife.

Last office party – too much booze
It went beyond the 'just good friend's'
They slipped away to her small flat.
He knows that soon he'll have to choose.

She brings out the protective streak
In him. He wants to make it right
But then imagines telling his
Two sons he's moving out next week.

And now his wife, who's cried about
The whole affair, is stressing how,
Although they've something special still,
He can't come back if he walks out.

Ironic – he would not have dreamt
His infidelity might cause
Her love for him to be revived –
Before she only felt contempt.

They pressure mounts, he must decide.
With ultimatums in the air,
Confusion growing day by day,
Conflicting feelings all collide.

He knows he's heading for The Crunch
(It's like a Big Bang in reverse)
All options closing down he's left
Anticipating next week's lunch.

Melvyn Rust
Runner Up, 1998

For the Rub

The lighter never   sparks
until the rub of thumb   a slight movement
gently clicks into position.
This is the only way it   will burn,
the only way to light   a cigarette.
This is the only way to rub.

Suppose it is as you suppose,
that I am that cigarette
between your lips   waiting
for the rub,
the click,
the flame   your face
branded on my brain,
I speak rain and of open air.

There is so much I have   forgotten lost
under the red sky   in the tilt of your car.
I have forgotten
about movement,
famished eyes,
loose and white
breasts growing
rounder
against the wind.

Nights   smell
empty and drastic.
I have forgotten   myself
in the middle
of sentences.

Where do words go   after
they are spoken?
I want your throat
I want to complicate   you,
divide your blood
from your skin.
Follow your scars   running
down your hands so
I will know before   you reach
how not   to touch.

Kathleen A. Karlis
Runner Up, 1998

Stone

Arched in praise against a holy sky,
paying penance laid on chapel floor,
buildings where we're born and live and die,
rusted by hinges holding history's door,
buttress where waves do battle with shore,
bridges we can cross the rivers by,
shelter for sheep on icy, wind-swept moor,
still and quiet where the witches lie,
in some ancient circle gathered round,
torn by metal monsters from the ground,
thrown in anger when the sirens sound,
placed in hope where loved ones lie alone,
keeper of fossil, feather, skin and bone,
cold, unseeing, silent traveller. Stone.

Louise Holmes
Yorkshire Prize, 1998

Lumb Bank, September 1998

Either take the Misery Lane via Bank,
or fast forward on the Victoria Line
or Piccadilly, stopping at King's Cross.
All other lines take years. The train to Leeds
leaves at midday. The working holiday
begins now. You arrive at Leeds on time

and change for the cross-country train, where time
goes backwards after Halifax, Lumb Bank
near Hebden Bridge, your final stop. Today
is Monday and the leaf-confettied line
that winds its way from Manchester to Leeds
to Manchester, is mad for it. Across

the carriage, a young girl flaunting a cross
and chain and purple lovebite asks the time,
nostalgic for her long weekend in Leeds.
End stop. Await a taxi to Lumb Bank,
meet more white knuckled poets, stand in line
and drink the vintage of the Yorkshire day,

expertly chilled. Leisurely seize the day,
unpack rough urban realism and cross
the threshold of taboo, the thick white line
that says 'no entry'. Suddenly, there's time
to find the path along the river bank
winking with baby blackberries, that leads

much further up the valley. Someone leads
discussion over dinner and today
you learn that Ted Hughes once lived at Lumb Bank
and that in Heptonstall beyond the cross
and stained glass memories, brittle with time,
Sylvia Plath engraves her final line.

Tomorrow you will learn where to place line
breaks, when to punctuate. Whoever leads
day three will teach you how to craft spare time
into poems. On Thursday witness day
break over a blank page. By Friday cross
your fingers for an encore of Lumb Bank.

This Saturday, you'll spend your measured time
(abandoning the crossword after Leeds)
editing Lumb Bank poems, line by line.

Patience Agbabi
Judge, 1998

The Dog

I called up Amazon dot Com and entered 'Robert Frost';
hoary name like a birch tree in a disco amongst the graphics.
Working down the list I spotted the cassette tapes
and bounced my electric order of the satellite to Seattle;
The tapes arrived shrink wrapped from their traverse
of the North Pole in the belly of a Boeing
and I took them on the M25 to Chelmsford.
Passing Potters Bar, with St. Albans Cathedral
a squat blue bedstead on the west horizon
I listened to 'Death of a Hired Man',
the tape unspooling that ponderous conversation;
Then just before the tunnel with ceiling tracer sodiums:
'Trees at my window, window tree, my sash is lowered..'
and behind and beyond the gravelly voice
a faint dog bark out in the Massachussets night.
It couldn't be caught, wouldn't be edited out;
barking at house lights maybe or a passing car
or rustlings from the dark shadows at the end of a yard.
It stayed with me in the Hanningfields,
in Wickford, the Baddows, Woodham Ferrers;
that defiant animus behind a mesh of wires.

Christopher North
Runner Up, 1998

Seven Triads

"Three things that enrich the poet:
>fables,
>poetic strength.
>A well of old verse."
>>- Triad, *The Red Book of Hergest*

Three enrichments of the poet's neck:
>that it be stocked with neck-verse,
>that it be harder than Kevlar,
>that giraffes have less.

Three things wisely kept back the first night:
>the chocolate sauce,
>the colonic irrigator,
>the sonnet novel.

Three more ways of turning bowels to sorbet:
>"Like to share a Toronto Blessing?"
>"Like to see Rodin's *Kiss* in earwax?"
>"Like to hear my new sestina?"

Three things poets secretly expect for their birthdays:
>gold
>frankincense,
>myrrh.

Three scratchings:
>scratch a bitter critic find a bitter writer,
>scratch a bitter writer find a blighted poet,
>scratch a blighted poet find yourself in Casualty.

Three classes the poet seeks reassurance from:
>the animal,
>the vegetable,
>the mineral.

Three arguments in favour of poets:
        the World,
        the Flesh,
        the Devil.

Ian Duhig, Editor

The Jigsaw Test

If you're not sure you know him well enough –
you think you know this guy but you're not sure –
try the jigsaw test:

nip down to Smith's and buy a thousand piece job
with lots of snow or flowers or clear blue sky
and bring it out one night;

tip the whole boxful on a shiny table
not large enough to lay them out face up;
when you've done the edge bits

and he's nose down, hooked into one small area,
stretch over for some pieces he's collected
and try to fit them in;

hog the picture on the lid and cry out
in triumph every time you put a piece in,
and pat that piece;

crunch slowly through a packet of ready salted,
if he gets sniffy drop some on the floor
and turn the heating up

and when it's nearly done, hide one or two bits
so you can fit the last piece in – make sure
he knows you did this.

If by this time he hasn't sworn, protested,
elbowed you, slagged you off about your breeding,
kicked the table over

and stormed off in a huff to see his mother –
just sits there looking chuffed with his achievement –
wish him goodnight, God bless,

then curl up with CD and your cat
and ask yourself, do you really want a bloke
who likes doing jigsaws?

Ken Hedger
Runner Up, 1998

Steven's Side

I am supporting Steven
as if I were a beam
      under his ceiling, even
though he is not a team.
      Under his ceiling even
a nightmare is a dream.

Steven and I have entered.
Some people have implied
      I would be too self-centred
to cheer for Steven's side,
      I would be too self-centred
to fail if Steven tried.

I am supporting Steven
as if I were a rail
      behind his curtain, even
though he is bound to fail.
      Behind his curtain even
a white net is a veil.

Steven is no performer.
He has no gift for sport.
      I make no cool crowd warmer
by staging my support.
      I make no cool crowd warmer,
adorn no tennis court

but I am supporting Steven
as if I were a pin
      above his hemline, even
though he will never win.
      Above his hemline even
a jacket is a skin.

I am supporting Steven.
I am at Steven's feet.
      I put him first and even
give him a thing to beat.
      I put him first and even
then he will not compete.

Sophie Hannah
Judge, 1998

Leaving You Behind

European Studies at Portsmouth P60
German and Social Policy at Leeds L14
Foreign Contemporary Issues as Goldsmith's College
(The University of London) G56

"So I'll be spending a year abroad then"
Your mouth opens. You're about to speak.
I know what you're thinking.

You hope I'll be alone in a bedsit on the 12th floor
and the lift is broken
and I'm scratching your name on a mouldy desk
and dodging junkies on the U-bahn.

You'll be happy when I enter a classroom of 38 german adolescents
and can't remember the word for pavement.

When I smile and tell the 82 year old neighbour she's a whore.
When I laugh at being called one myself
by the 38 adolescents
and they laugh even more.

When it's been 3 months
and I'm still waiting to get my luggage back from Cuba.

When my brolly breaks.
Es regnet wieder.

The deaf 82 year old has left her T.V. on
at full volume. I can't sleep

and I can't remember the word for pavement.

When I'm being corrected on my knowledge
of the Ancient Anglo-feudal system.
When I'm being asked about the annual British expenditure for bread.
How the fuck should I know?

"But you have been from England, don't you"

When all I want's a postage stamp
But I can't, for the life and death of me,
remember the word for pavement
and this is a disaster to me.

When I miss home
and I've got no friends
except for Lederhosen Sven who keeps asking me,
"Do I like Wienna?"

When I miss home
and I miss you
and I'm wishing I never left you alone

When it's all my own fault
you're now engaged to Zoe
and you're happy
and her and her cat have moved in
and you've got a nice cozy dwelling
in the hollow of her head
snuggled up with Smoky!

When I can't remember the German for pavement
and I can't remember the English for Friedhof.

and you can't remember my name.

Susan Brown
ilf Young Writers Prize, 1998

accidents with time & numbers

1 /

I called the number by accident the first time. It was not the last
His wife answered, a warm unknowing hello to a perfect stranger
Disorientated as separated worlds collided. I hung up, gasped
The numbers had fired-off in my hand like a gun
For three years in-law we were father and son
Life's full of accidents, usually in the home
They felt cheated, betrayed. It's understood
Quickly it paled, thinned to water, the kind that flows under bridges
Once it was almost blood

2 /

Even with his back turned he's 6 feet 2, silver haired, wiry but strong
From the front there's a beard through which he'd giggle
At his family and his friends, his sharp mind made for good times
He had a superstition, he never said goodbye, just 'seeya'
If his parents were mentioned, it would not normally be by him
He would mask reverence in shiny eyes

Jazz is his passion blue notes sing his name
Trumpets, clarinets and double bass
Art, Bird and Monk number his friends
I bought some of his music to play in my new life
Just sounds, they clash around the house, the colours far too bright
I suspect the Cool School play reluctantly
For me and my soon to be, new wife

3 /

I heard he's a grandad by his other daughter, and I bet he's 63
Retired maybe if he stuck to his plan, and maybe
There's a new man sitting with his youngest in the comfy seats
Breathing in soft family and Sunday joints of meat
A new man who won't make the same mistakes as me
Falling for another but still wanting to hear Dizzy Gillespie

He once told me how many rolls of neck fat it took to make
A boogie-woogie piano player complete
Now shamed, I can't remember whether it's 6, 5, 4 or 3?

4/

Rugby on a Sunday and that night we'd drink, thick as thieves
I loved the way his mind worked
Throwing away the chaff, but caring for the weeds
Good company, generous, so much younger than his age
He'd never suffer racists, courageous in thought and deed
A gifted artist though he'd say his eye had gone
Every inch a man to admire, my best friend whom I loved
There I've said it and still I feel damned

5/

So it's goodbye not seeya
And I cannot blame him for my indiscretion
But parting is not the all, only the last
Because time is not forever, only what you catch
And you catch it forever, when it makes you care

No the parting is not my concern here
I just miss the easy, the clever, the values, the fun
I just miss, the so close, the almost being his son
And I ache to know how many rolls of neck fat
Make a boogie-woogie piano player a real Hep Cat.

John d. Senior
Runner Up, 1998

Bridge

Listen. The wind has backed north-east
filling with salt and sleet,
it scours the iron traceries –
God's wire brush and stripper –
paintwork blisters, scabs and flakes.

March to late September
we'd paint from shore to shore,
one equinoctial gale to clock us on,
one to sign us off to winter quarters,
two sentences, six months suspended.

A masterpiece of civil engineering,
Caledonia's greatest folly;
a Sisyphean torture spiced
with sea-salt and vertigo;
a net to catch the weather.

They found me painting in the dark
as if to foil the calendar
or tick a little faster than the clock
and cross the space before the bridge itself.

Peter Wakefield
Runner Up, 1998

Bacchanal

Here, on this ancient, hump-backed bridge in Bruges,
We lean together, looking at the swans
On the canal, Webbed water ripples, laps the refuge
Walls: the Begijnhof. Like Benedictine nuns

Or bridges coquetting in the moonlight's mystery,
They glide, a stately argosy, full-blown
As cabbage roses, silent at midnight on this day
Of Valentine. The lacemakers are gone

Now, the Beguines, the pious sisterhood
Under religious rule, slumbering beneath
The flagstones in their church of scented wood,
Sleeping the long, sequestered sleep of death

Within the cloister's confine. In the oak-beamed,
Burnished, restaurant on Wijngaardsplein,
Where, by the fire, Vermeer and Brueghel would have seemed
At home, we dined on *frites* and *mosselen*,

On *carbonade flamande, aardbei* and Trappist cheese.
Later, we drank the champagne air and walked
Along the cobbled street, the evening breeze
Fanning our cheeks. We neither talked

Nor needed to. Now, arm-in-arm, we stop and lean
Against the parapet, the waxing February moon
Sailing on silk beneath us on the feast of Valentine,
Our thirty third, ending contentedly, in quietness, soon.

Norman Bissett
Runner Up, 1998

Moving On

After you returned from Athens, you said,
Living in England was like living in a wet lettuce,
So green and damp, with soft, leaf-cut light,
So different from the harsh contrasts of Greece,
Flaring scarlet flowers that trumpeted the sun,
Sea that shimmered like a mirage on hot tarmac,
Sunlight glittering on the columns of Pericles:
The passion and the anger and the grief, from which
You fled with your grandmother's jewellery
And two half-Greek, twin children, all
Illegally exported. You left behind
A Greek family, robbed of its grandchildren,
Of its precious blood-line, simmering
With rage and cursing you through mutual friends.

You left behind trunks, too, full of family things:
Your father's medals, who, as pilot of a Swordfish,
Was first to sight the *Bismark*, silhouettes
Of forgotten ancestors in blind profile,
Dingy oil-paintings of estates long-sold
Some heavy silver plate, handed down
Through centuries, now perhaps
Melted down into anonymous ingots.

The month the children were conceived
You drove into the Greek hinterland with your lover
To visit Delphi, and among the barren mountains
The twins began their tortuous journey
Into life, and though no oracle could foretell
The windings of their journey, or of yours,
You knew then that your life in Greece was withering
Just as surely as you knew the moment of conception.

The twins have moved on in their wandering constellation;
Charlotte is in Japan now, teaching English;
At weekends she climbs Mount Fuji or picnics
Under peach-blossom. Ewan, meanwhile,
Learns Danish in dour Copenhagen.
Charlotte has the straight, haughty nose
Of a marble Aphrodite, Ewan, the tousled black curls
That a stone Apollo can only suggest. Both
Speak Greek, but both have learned it
From text books: they do not remember the Greek
They spoke at play in the streets of Athens,
Or to their father, when they were little children.

One abiding memory, for you, is of Greek drivers,
Sun flashing from their windshields,
Leaning out of their side windows, their arms
Slicing the air with karate-chops of contempt,
Eyebrows high with disbelief, mouths agape with fury.

Everything here is so sedate, you say;
People stay indoors, bite their tongues,
Brood. Though they are polite enough,
They don't like foreigners, don't readily accept
Refugees like yourself. There is nowhere now
Where you do not feel a stranger.

                              The place
We feel is ours, which welcomes us
With voices and with gestures that we recognise
As our own, is perhaps where first our feelings
Were focused like rays of sun through a lens.
For you, I suppose, it was Greece. Somewhere,
Maybe, among the winding roads
Of the arid Greek hinterland, on the way
To Delphi, where love burned so fiercely
That only ash was left to drift in the dry grass,
And yet the buds of twin flowers first began
Uncoiling into life.

Now you are settled
In damp England, pottering in the garden
At weekends, where weeds unravel in the dark soil
And in the morning sometimes, beaded webs
Of gossamer lace the lawn. Yesterday, a fine mist
Hid the spires of the ruined Abbey
Where we walked among the ancient graves
Looking for mossy stones in whose blurred lettering
Might be made out the names of your forebears.

Jonathan Brown
Runner Up, 1998

No north or south

(the ghosts of Luddites wait in ambush for walkers in woods intending to
smash their compasses)

"As you were!" the leaf mould whispers.
and this morning we are still wet dark,
uttering our last gutteral;
saliva, like a dew drop, hangs
on chin stubble from York gallows.

Through the waste and moorland we came,
one place deferring to the next
twinkling skyline; sometimes smoke
from mills presumed to crop the moon.
Factories grab light from the world.

Our blacked-up shadows rustle, stalking
anoraks of man-made fibre,
the weave of lies. They go straight,
like shuttles, through these shifting woods
deaf to its whispering, minding

their small compass machine...
a queer glass an an arrow within
that ruthlessly scratches the North.
I don't know why it teasles so
but always it's a nit at my back

Their master's plot borrows Ludd's
trickery, a Flavio Gioia of Amalfi
could not be shot as he was not,
but secretly, from a workshop
the compasses came putting the stars

out of work, carding wild fleurs-de-lys
and twisting our faith in the places
we might not know... My clog heel crushes
glass, and wood smiths the arrow until,
it points clearly, steadily, to itself.

Bruce Barnes
First Prize, 1998

Closure

We shake our heads and rue
first leaf litter as if
it had never been before
& the story was new

but where you come from
it's dark always & there
you will return soon, late,
whatever I plot or

ascribe; I'm what you wrote,
once, as a kid when you tried
out the other hand
& found a wobbly likeness,

an opposite, but one
you couldn't count on,
the line, the season, untrue
& yet your own.

Tracy Ryan
Judge, 1998

Saturation

It is between my fingers
and behind my knees,

on the soles of my feet,
under my arms where the hair is dark

and in the knotted dip of my navel.
It stiffens my joints and lower spine,

invades my blood and the cells
of my tracheoles,

is the cause of thumping
in the canals of my ears,

forms ninety percent of my eyes.
It sits in droplets on the face of my watch

and in the glass on the table
it is the very tension of the meniscus.

In the fibres of the linen sheets,
it lingers as it does in the porcelain basin,

in the stems and the leaves
of the double headed geraniums,

in the gutter blocked with moss.
Everywhere except my lips

and the roof of my mouth,
which are dry, cracked and abraded

by the raw, sea saw of air,
in and out, in and out, the taste

of telling you, again and again,
this has got to stop.

S. Butler
Second Prize, 1998

Biography

Editor
Name	Ian Duhig
Born	1954, London
Now Lives	Leeds
Occupation	Poet

1998 Judge
Name	Tracy Ryan
Born	1964, Perth, Western Australia
Now Lives	Cambridge
Occupation	Visiting Fellow at Robinson College, Cambridge

1998 Judge
Name	Sophie Hannah
Born	1971, Manchester
Now Lives	Saltaire and Cambridge
Occupation	Fellow Commoner in Creative Arts, Trinity College, Cambridge

1998 Judge
Name	Patience Agbabi
Born	1965, London
Now Lives	London
Occupation	Poet, performer and workshop facilitator

1994 Judge
Name	Matthew Sweeney
Born	1952, Donegal
Now Lives	London
Occupation	Poet

1994 Prize Winner
Name	Stephanie Bowgett
Born	1950, Slough
Now Lives	Huddersfield
Occupation	Writer and Part-Time Teacher

1995 Judge
Name	Ian McMillan
Born	1956, Darfield, Barnsley
Now Lives	Darfield, Barnsley
Occupation	Writer, Broadcaster and Man About Town

1995 Prize Winner & 1998 Winner, 3rd Prize
Name   John Latham
Born   1937, Frodsham
Now Lives   Warrington
Occupation   Freelance writer and physicist

1996 Judge
Name   Vernon Scannell
Born   1922
Now Lives   Otley
Occupation   Poet

1996 Prize Winner
Name   David Duncombe
Born   1935, Coventry
Now Lives   Matlock
Occupation   Writer/Teacher

1997 Judge
Name   UA Fanthorpe
Born   1929
Now Lives   Wotton-Under-Edge
Occupation   Poet

1997 Winner
Name   Louise Goulding
Born   1975, Bradford
Now Lives   Bradford
Occupation   Just Graduated

Student Prize
Name   Amy Fidgett
Born   1983, Chelmsford
Now Lives   Ilkley
Occupation   GCSE Student, Ilkley Grammar School

1998 Winner, 1st Prize
Name   Bruce Barnes
Born   1948, Leytonstone, London
Now Lives   Bradford
Occupation   Bradford Council Housing Officer and Poet

1998 Winner, 2nd Prize
Name	Sue Butler
Now Lives	Wymondham, Norfolk

ilf Young Poet
Name	Susan Brown
Born	1981, York
Now Lives	York
Occupation	A Level Student - All Saints, York

Yorkshire Prize
Name	Louise Holmes
Born	1957, Bradford
Now Lives	Idle, Bradford
Occupation	Married with two children, writer of poetry, fiction and freelancer for greetings cards

Runners Up
Name	Jonathan Brown
Born	1946, Bristol
Now Lives	York
Occupation	Project Manager, Park Lane College, Leeds

Name	John d Senior
Born	1964, Dewsbury
Now Lives	Ossett
Occupation	Compositor

Name	Peter Wakefield
Born	1953, Wolverhampton
Now Lives	Cononley, Keighley
Occupation	Counsellor and Poet

Name	Kathleen A Karliss
Born	1950, Salem, Ohio, USA
Now Lives	Leeds
Occupation	English Teacher and Poet

Name	S W Rydderch
Born	1966, Aberystwyth
Now Lives	Newquay
Occupation	Administration

Name   Christopher North
Born   1945, South London
Now Lives   Chalfont St Giles, Buckinghamshire
Occupation Surveyor

Name   Melvyn Rust
Born   1950, London
Now Lives   St Albans
Occupation Computer Consultant working towards being a poet

Name   Norman Bissett
Born: 1938, Fife
Now Lives   Edinburgh
Occupation: Retired British Council

Name   Ken Hedger
Born   1930, Eastleigh, Hampshire
Now Lives   Ellerton, York
Occupation Retired Social Worker and Poet

Name   Dorothy V Pope
Born   1935, Plymouth, Devon
Now Lives   Harrow On The Hill
Occupation English Teacher